Pikmi Pops Surprise!

The Missing Easter Bunny

By Jenne Simon

Illustrated by Artful Doodlers Ltd.

SO CUTE

All rights reserved. Published by Scholastic Inc., *Publishers since 1920*. SCHOLASTIC and associated logos are trademarks and/or registered trademarks of Scholastic Inc.

The publisher does not have any control over and does not assume any responsibility for author or third-party websites or their content.

This book is a work of fiction. Names, characters, places, and incidents are either the product of the author's imagination or are used fictitiously, and any resemblance to actual persons, living or dead, business establishments, events, or locales is entirely coincidental.

ISBN 978-1-338-31607-0

10 9 8 7 6 5 4 3 2 1   19 20 21 22 23

Printed in the U.S.A.   40

First printing 2019

Book design by Becky James

SCHOLASTIC INC.

Ebby the Bunny had invited all the Pikmis for an Easter egg hunt.
"Who's ready to find the Easter eggs?" barked Pichi.
"Me! Me!" squeaked Gizmit. "I'm an egg-hunting machine!"
"Last one to fill their basket is a rotten egg," said Leroy.

But there was one problem. Ebby was nowhere to be found!

"Hmm," said Fetti. "While I was picking the purr-fect raspberries, I did notice Ebby acting a little mysterious."

The other Pikmis had, too.
Bibble saw Ebby clean up a big mess.

Pichi had spotted Ebby lurking in the meadow.

Wubbs spied Ebby looking like a ghost in the middle of the night.

And Leroy had noticed Ebby burying something in the garden.

Then Fetti and Pichi found a puzzling note posted to one of the biggest, most colorful candy trees in Pikmi Land. It was from Ebby!

Ebby's Easter Egg Hunt

Ebby's Easter Egg Hunt

Welcome, dear Pikmis! You're in for a treat.
This Easter egg hunt is going to be sweet!
Your baskets are empty, but won't be for long—
If you follow the stars, you won't go wrong.
The first one to find me will win something great,
So hunt for eggs quickly—
and don't be late!

When: Sunday afternoon
Where: All over Pikmi Land
Prize: Wait and see!

All the Pikmis wanted to win the hunt—and the big prize. They looked high and low, and found pretty, painted Easter eggs in the most surprising places. But they still couldn't find Ebby.

"Maybe we have to wait until the stars come out tonight," said Pichi.
"That's clever!" said Leroy. "But Ebby's note said the hunt is this afternoon."

"Maybe Ebby is hiding in the garden," suggested Fetti.

The Pikmis looked under every lollipop, leaf, and petal. They found Easter eggs in the gumdrop bush, under the sprinkle rocks, and near the chocolate waterfall, yet no Ebby.

Then Gizmit spotted something round and purple buried among the lollipop bushes.

"Look!" cried Gizmit. "This egg is marked with stars!"

"It must be a clue to where Ebby is!" Pichi cried.

The Pikmis opened the egg . . . and sure enough, there was a note from Ebby inside!

"Berries in jars!" said Fetti. "I know where we can find that!"
Fetti led the other Pikmis to a tree house.

Sure enough, hidden among the lollipop branches and berries in jars was a blue Easter egg with more stars on it!

"You're a genius!" Wubbs told Fetti.

Fetti read the next clue.

Where green is made from yellow and blue, a true masterpiece is waiting for you!

"Oh! I know! I know!" said Bibble. "There's a secret spot outside where you can mix colors and create masterpieces!"

The Pikmis found clay and brushes and pencils and paints. But no egg.
Then Bibble remembered the clue.

"When I dye my wool, I mix yellow and blue to make green. The egg we're looking for must be painted green!"

Clever Ebby! The egg was hidden in plain sight!

"Where could that be?" wondered Gizmit. "It's getting late. The hunt is almost over!"

The Pikmis were stumped. What happened if no one won? But then Pichi spotted a mark on the floor.

"That looks like Ebby's footprint!" cried Pichi.

"You're a real Sherlock Bones!" said Wubbs.

"If we hurry, we just might win Ebby's big prize," said Fetti.
"Then let's bunny-hop-to-it!" twittered Gizmit.
The Pikmis ran along the pink trail as fast as their paws would carry them.

Finally, the Pikmis reached the end of the paw print trail.

"It's an Easter tea party!" cried Bibble. "For all of us to enjoy!"

WEL

"So this is what Ebby has been planning," said Fetti. "It must have taken a lot of work!"

"What a squeak-heart!" said Gizmit.

"This is the most egg-cellent Easter egg hunt ever!" gushed Leroy.

"But where *is* Ebby?" asked Pichi.

Ebby wasn't under the tea table or hiding behind the flowers.

Then they noticed the giant chocolate egg in the corner.
Was it . . . bouncing?
The chocolate egg cracked in two, and out popped Ebby!
"Looks like we *all* found you!" said Pichi.
"So it looks like we all get the prize," added Gizmit.

"Prize? Every bunny knows that the sweetest prize is a sur-prize," Ebby said with a wink. "So here it is—you get to plan the Easter egg hunt next year!"

All the Pikmis laughed. What a surprise indeed!

"*Hoppy* Easter, Ebby!" they cheered.

"Hoppy Easter, friends!" Ebby replied.